Sleep, My Bunny

ROSEMARY WELLS

WALKER BOOKS
AND SUBSIDIARIES
LONDON · BOSTON · SYDNEY · AUCKLAND

The owls
and crickets
are singing
together.

The night wind
has taken
the moon for
a ride.

The first rain
of summer
is bending
the heather,

as soft as
a feather,
I hear it
outside.

Hush now,
you hoot owls,
and crickets,
be wary –

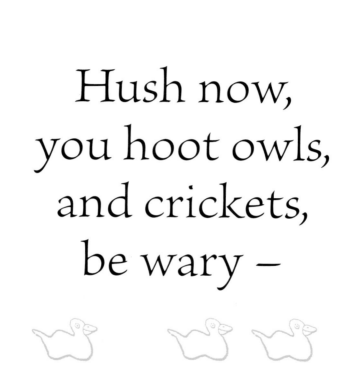

the morning
is hiding
behind the
next cloud.

May the noises
of evening
be gentle
and airy.

Let nothing
be scary
and nothing
be loud.

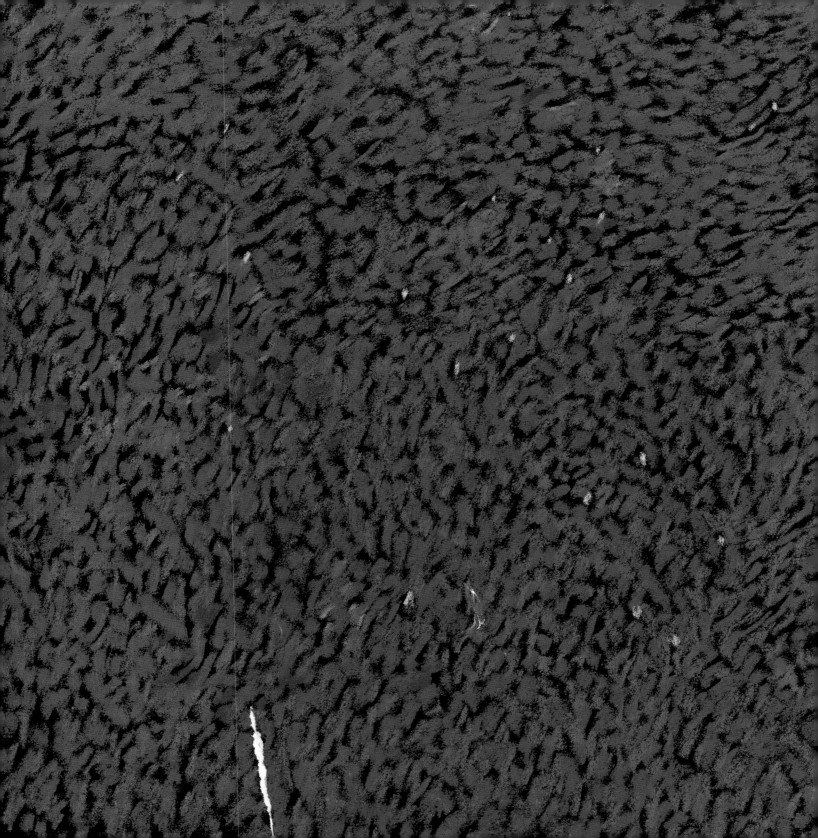

For Frances, who helped!

First published in Great Britain 2019 by Walker Books Ltd, 87 Vauxhall Walk, London SE11 5HJ • © 1977, 2018 Rosemary Wells • Text previously published as "Good Night, Sweet Prince" in *Don't Spill It Again, James* by Rosemary Wells. • The right of Rosemary Wells to be identified as author and illustrator of this work has been asserted by her in accordance with the Copyright, Designs and Patents Act 1988 • This book has been typeset in Brioso Pro • Printed in China • British Library Cataloguing in Publication Data: a catalogue record for this book is available from the British Library • ISBN 978-1-4063-8258-7 • www.walker.co.uk • 10 9 8 7 6 5 4 3 2 1